Little Doms

Carla Kopf

Contents

ONE.

The year is 2996 the world went through some major changes, vampires are now a thing.

Humans aren't enslaved well maybe just a little, at the age of 16 all humans get tested mentally and divided into categories: Dom/Sub, Daddy/Little, Mommy/little, Master/Pet, Master/slave.

If you aren't a dominant you are definitely a sub, its how the world work now, your Dom will take the role of providing you and taking care of you. Most people are spoiled although abuse does exist, the punishment of abusing your sub of any category is public execution.

So where the vampire role came you might ask, after their coming out five hundred years ago and bloody war between them and us human, the vampires manufactured a chemical gas that makes you go to a sub or Dom headspace and blew the world with it. They then signed a truce contract with the world's most dominants and here we are now. Humans and vampires get paired together for life, it can be a two vampire or two human pairings or it can be a mixed-race and mixed gender.

Ohh where are my manners I didn't introduce myself my name is Sophia, I'm 15 and three quarters. My Bday is next month and I'm not excited in fact I'm not looking forward to it at all. I'm 5 feet tall and weigh around 90 pounds I'm a bit underweight, I got brown hair and brown eyes, I'm nothing special.

I get bullied daily in my school just for being me, I know I'm not a dom, but I had no idea what kind of sub I am either. I'm too afraid of being a slave that doesn't seem fun, not fun at all. Maybe being a regular sub will be good for me, but I do have very little pain intolerance. Okay so that leaves me with either being a pet or a little, those two are my best choices.

I'm too taken by my own thoughts to notice where I'm going that until I hit a human wall and my worst nightmare. I DID NOT JUST HIT Andy Baraghani (if you watch bon appetite on YouTube you'll know who he is)

"What do you think you're doing" ~Andy "I'm sorry...I'm sorry...I didn't mean to..." ~Sophia Something burned my face it took me a moment to understand he just slapped me, took hold of my hair, and pinned me against a wall with my back toward him. "Watch it little thing...you'll be sixteen soon and I might just make you mine" ~Andy

With that final statement he walked away, I ran toward the girl's bathroom crying my eyes out, I skipped my class too busy crying. I didn't stop crying till I vomited everything in my stomach, I decided to take advantage and go to the nurse's office to see how red my eyes are, how pale my face is and the fact that I just vomited she might let me go home early.

She did let me go, it was almost the end of the school year only a month yet to go, we weren't learning much, most people knew by now if they are dominant or submissive not me yet.

The walk home was full with my sniffles, thinking about having Andy as my Dom, he'll probably just beat me for fun. His parents are both vampires and his dad is known to be a very alpha male, his mother was a human when she gave birth to him but got changed later, he'll get changed too at eighteen after he chose his permanent sub.

I made it home and went straight to my room, my parents were both human, my dad died when I was ten in a car accident and my mother is a retailer, she was the Dom of their relationship, and seeing her only daughter a sub is a big disappointment for her.

In a month time, I'll be tested, then they'll choose what kind of institutions to send me to, they are all Dom/Sub school like an institution, I'll still learn math, English, and this academic stuff but add to that I'll take subs classes, and I'll have an appointed dom.

The doms chose who they want, anyone that's left gets appointed a substitute Dom till the next batch of sub and doms arrives.

You can reject a Dom well if you are brave enough and can break it off if things don't go the way you wanted. Physical examination is mandatory to make sure no one is getting abused.

The vampires aren't allowed to drink directly from their sub until they are official and are together forever, there are blood donors and bagged blood for them.

I close my eyes and try to sleep, thinking about the future and all that's to come is giving me a headache.

TWO.

- -

Today is the day I've been waiting for...not. It's my Bday and I can't be any more miserable, I woke up to someone shaking me and taking off my blanket. "Sophia better wake up before I whip that ass of yours," the voice says and I try to ignore it, that until I feel a sharp slap on my butt and I jump up.

I look to whom it was who wakes me and I see it's my mother she's wearing her no-nonsense face, dressed in her tailored suit, my mother is 5'5 and well-built she's blond with green eyes, I had all my looks from my dad and she hates me even more for it.

"You got thirty minutes to be ready, I'm taking you to the classification center," my mother says and leaves the room.

I feel tears burning my eyes but I ignore them, I wasn't expecting a hug and a kiss but a happy Bday would have been enough, knowing that she's not someone to mess with I get up and get ready in twenty-five minutes I give myself a mental hurray.

Well my mother wasn't impressed she walked straight to her car not giving me a chance to grab breakfast, the drive was silent and I was okay with it. The only time I and my mother talk is when she yells at me or beats me.

The classification center is a big building, the inside is all sterile and looks like a hospital. My mother goes to the front desk and gives them my name, showing my ID, you could wait up to three months after your sixteen birthday to be classified but my mother decided to make me do it on the same day.

She probably can't wait to get rid of me, it's a miracle she hasn't put me up for adoption after the first time I came home bloodied, I was eight and Andy his friends hit me for the first time, I came home crying dad took care of me and kissed all my bruises while my mother stood disapproving saying I should've hit back and stood for myself.

I was so taken by my thoughts that I didn't notice my name being called, I'm doing that too often getting lost in my own head. Mother pinched my thigh and it really hurt I looked up to the nurse that was calling me, I felt like crying but doing that will insure a real beating from her.

The nurse takes me to an examination room, I get a physical exam, and I have a few bruises on my body but not enough to raise alarm. They all passed under the "I fell" and "I'm clumsy" excuse. They inform me that I'm underweight but other than that I'm in good health.

They got me ready for the mental examination a psychologist sit along with me and ask me a few general questions about if I'm happy, what do I want to be, do I miss my dad, I'm I a daddy or mommy girl, do I self-harm.

I answered her honestly I'm not happy but I'm not sad either, I had no idea what I want to be and I miss my dad so much it hurts, I was definitely my daddy girl and no I don't self-harm mother does a great job on me, no need to add to my bruises and scars.

I finally get injected with the same chemical that caused this whole mess in the world and I get attached to a stimulator. It's like a dream, I see myself moving I see my father, mother I even see Andy, my tormentor. But just like a dream I can't remember any details by the time the stimulator is taken off, they tell me to sit and rest. I have a headache and feel disoriented.

My mother is led to my room, she enters with a vampire doctor who got my result.

"Miss Sophia, 16 years old. Daughter of Emmanuel Monroe "the doctor asks and I nod.

No one uses their last name before they are classified, if you are a Dom you use your parent's last name, if you are a sub you'll have to wait till you get a Dom and use their last name.

"Sophia, you are classified as a submissive, little girl, little age 2, we recommend a vampire Dom with the ability to be changed, later on, you will be sent to the Dom/Little institution in DC. If you have any objection you got two weeks to file a complaint, you are expected in the institution in a week. Any question"

I look at the doctor weirdly, I'm a little??? My age going to be two?? I'll be a toddler and they recommend a VAMPIRE DADDY FOR MEEEE!!!!

I didn't even get the chance to reply before my mother spoke.

"I'll sign all her papers now, you can send her to hell for all I care," she says to the doctor and then turns to me "you are no daughter of mine rot in hell" with that she turns on her heel and leave.

Well, I was expecting to be abounded by her but disowned, that's cold even for her. I can't help the tears that flow freely down my face now.

The nice doctor turns to me and tries to calm me saying he'll call the school and can get settled there tonight, that's one of the best schools and I won't need a thing. I nod to him but my tears keep on coming.

THREE.

The doctor was right the school did send someone to get me but they sent two vampires. I was kind of scared of them they were both around 6 feet tall, a girl and a guy they were both blond and have similar eye colors, sibling's maybe.

"Hello little one we are here to take you to your new home," the guy says. "I'm time and this is Tasha, she's going to help you change to something more comfortable then we'll go okay," the guy says again and I nod my head yes, I was still in the hospital gown they gave me before my physical exam.

Tasha took me to a bathroom she washed my face and pulled a bag for me, it looks like I'm not getting back into my jeans and shirt. She gets pull-ups from the bag and I shake my head no, I'm a big girl.

"Come on pet it's a long drive back, just in case you had an accident" Tasha tries to reason with me, but I don't want it I try to run away from her. Well, a big mistake since she's a vampire and much faster than a normal human being, she moved faster than I could follow landed two slaps on my butt, and pulled the pull-ups on me. Once again I was in tears, she continued to dress me ignoring my tears she put me in some baby blue onesie and baby pink overall and finished the look with some converse and pink socks.

She took my hand and guided me back toward Timy "ready to go? Did she give you any troubles" he asked eyeing my tear blotched face. "None I couldn't handle" she replied and we left the classification center, it was late in the afternoon. We got into an SUV, they sat me in the back and buckled me in.

"Take a nap little one it's a long drive home" ~Timmy I cried a bit more as we left the only town and the only house I knew, it wasn't all happy memories but I had all my memories with dad here. After crying for about an extra hour I did fell asleep.

The next time I woke up it was in a MacDonald drive through with Tasha shaking me " pet you want a burger or chicken nuggets" I replied chicken nuggets with my eyes still half-closed, are we there yet. Timy hand me my food with a warning not to get his car dirty. I did my best eating only landing a few ketchup drops on my clothes but not on the car.

After an extra thirty-minute drive we make it, the school is a giant castle that's been renewed to be a school, it's all made of stone with some gargoyles status, it was creepy in the dark.

"Home sweet home," they say together as we drive in, Timmy Park in a private marked by his name Timy Vitale.

I knew that name, they are a well-known vampire family, and they are all doms. They are also known in the mafia world, they are one of the scariest family and no one dares to mess with them.

Tasha and Timmy took a hand each and walked me to some kind of dorm, the room is all in pastel colors with stuffies on the bed, a desk with a laptop on top of it, a walk-in closet full of clothes and school uniform, and an adjacent bathroom.

"This is your room till someone adopt you, then you'll move in with your dom" ~Tasha I nod my head, I'm tired from crying all day, and even after my nap in the car I'm still tired, well I guess being a little won't be that bad.

Tasha went into the closet while Timmy started to undress me, I tried fighting him saying I can do it but he just shook his head and stripped me, Tasha came back with some pajama, Timmy dressed me in my pajama after he took the pull-ups off and putting some cotton panty on for me, can I blush more than I am? No, I doubt.

After I'm embarrassed to death they tuck me in bed, saying I'm going to have a big day tomorrow.

Somehow I did have some extra tears to shed before I fell asleep.

FOUR.

I woke up to Tasha shaking me awake gently and laying a few kisses on my face, that's new nobody woke me this gently this my dad died. Tasha is alone today well thank god, I don't want Timmy to change my clothes again, she sends me to the shower and I'm grateful I get to do it alone, I brushed my teeth and she brushed my hair for me, even put it in two pigtails.

"This little uniform, if you see someone wearing it then he or she is a little," she says while lying on my bed in a dark blue plaid skirt with a white shirt and a blue tie.

"Doms wear a full-on suit just watch the ties blue is for a daddy or mommy, black is for a Dom, green for a Master for pet and red is Master and slave, other subs wear a uniform like yours but the color differ depend on their categories got it?" she asks and I just nod trying to file all these information for later use.

She drags me off to what she says is Madame P.'s office she's the dean of this institute, a vampire and a Dom. I walk with Tasha feeling a bit scared, it's all too new for me. We reach a dark oak door and she knocks, there was a loud "come in".

Inside sat a beautiful woman her hair was up in a perfect bun she had some makeup on but it only intensifies her beauty, she looked young around thirty-ish but vampires stop aging at the age they've been made at, she's probably ancient but her beauty will never fade. I was too taken by her feature her gold eyes, blond hair, plump lips. Well, I'm straight as an arrow but I can appreciate beauty.

"Thank you, Tasha, that'll be all," she says and Tasha leaves the room, where did she goes and left me, I was starting to feel safe with her.

"Why don't you take a seat Sophia, we're going to have a quick chat" ~Madame P.

I nod my head and sit down Madame P takes her seat behind her desk, she looks at me for a minute then starts.

"Welcome to Dom and littles school Sophia, I'm the head master here, you can call me Mama P. most little do, now your file was sent to me with some big recommendations to accept you here.

We don't accept many subs or doms this school is kind of special some might say it's more of an elite school"

I just sit and listen nodding my head, I had no idea this place was special I thought I would be sent to a regular school, not to an elite one.

"Your classification test showed some great potential, We vampires live for a very very long time and these days it's getting more and more rare to find true littles.

I already enrolled you in required classes along with some DDLG classes.

You have till the end of this week so roam free by Friday we'll see any potential doms that want to adopt you as their little girl. You are free to reject or break up with a Dom if you two don't work well together or if you get abused.

If you get in any problems come straight to me, your grades are really important so don't disappoint me or there would be consequences"

Again I just nod, it's too much information for me to take.

"Would you like a daddy or a mommy Dom" she asks and I mumble a daddy. "I can't hear you little girl talk don't mumble" she scolds me

"Daddy please," I say quietly.

"Well of course my sweet little girl, now here's your schedule Timmy will you to your first class" she finishes.

I look down at my schedule I have the regular academic classes, gym (yuck), and two new classes for me little class and Dom and little class.

Timy walks into the office offers me his hand and we walk together toward my first class of the day, I'm scared and nervous it's a little class, I have no idea what's this about.

We enter a classroom it's full of littles wearing the same uniform as me, some daddy and mommy doms, the tables are two big round tables with chairs around them.

Timy hand me a pastel blue backpack I didn't notice he was carrying it, he said it got my stuff in it. He gives me a kiss on the forehead tells me to have fun and make new friends before he leaves.

I'm frozen in place till a bell ring and the doms leave the room, a woman with kind eyes comes toward me.

"You must be Sophia my new student" oww she must be my teacher, I just nod my head yes.

"I'm Miss Blair, go put your stuff in the cupboard that has your name on it and then come sit with the rest of the class," my teacher says and I obey.

I'm sitting next to a guy who's as short as me which is funny since we are the two shortest people in the class and probably in the whole school. I gave him a shy smile and he smiles back and gives my hand a little squeeze.

Turn out little class is the class where you learn all about being little, how to regress, how to cope emotionally, about the pacifier, bottles, diapers all this embarrassing stuff.

FIVE.

After my first class was over the kind boy who sat next to me introduced himself. "Hello I'm Rory," he said and stick his hand out for me to shake "Hello Rory I'm Sophia," I say while shaking his hand. "You're new here?" ~Rory "Yeah it's my first day" ~Sophia "Let me see your schedule," he asks and I hand him my schedule

"Oww oww, we got almost everything together. Wanna be my friend I've been here for two weeks and the other kids are mean to me cause my age is young" ~Rory

"Yes I would love to" I couldn't help it, he was adorable "how old are you"

He holds three fingers for me, oww he meant he's regression age, if he's three and everyone is mean to him what will they do to me.

"What about you," he asks and I lift two fingers he gives me a sympathetic look and a hug well at least now I have a friend.

The day passes quickly I have most classes with Rory except English and PE. I'm walking out of my English class which sucked since there were so many doms there with me and I was the only little, they all gave me weird looks as if they wanted to eat me alive.

I was half walking half running out of the class and toward the cafeteria when I hit someone, I start apologizing to whoever I hit, the first thing I notice it's a dom with a black tie, I look up at his face and I see my worst nightmare.

Not it can't be true. I'm looking eye to eye with Andy my own personal bully from my old school, he's been MIA for the last few weeks but I was so busy fretting about my bday to notice or enjoy it.

"Look what we have here," he says and pins toward the wall "They made you a little? Hmm, I always thought you'd be a good slave but oh well" he said before gripping my hair and pulling on it making me crane my neck up with our eyes meeting. "I don't care who you fucked or blew to get here little slut but you better stay away from me or I'll make your life a living hell got me," he says and I nod. He slam my head against the wall and ask again "got me?" he wants words it's one of his twisted games if I want to live I have to play along so I whisper "yes sir" he laughs and lets me go.

I start running away from him while crying this brought back so many bad memories, he always made me cry till I vomited. I needed somewhere to hide a bathroom would be great right now.

I'm still looking for a restroom when someone hand snake around my waist and I'm pulled toward a powerful chest. I look up, way up, this guy is about 6 feet tall and I'm met with kind green eyes, he's wearing a blue tie and suit so I know he's a daddy dom.

"What's got a little angel like you crying and running," he says try to wipe my tears but I shy away.

"Oww you must be new here, are the big bad doms scaring you," he says in a baby voice and I nod, I don't know if he's making fun of me or trying to help.

"Okay little girl let's get some yummy to your tummy," he says and starts dragging me toward the cafeteria, I missed breakfast this morning and I am hungry but I wasn't ready to go to the cafeteria where all the big bad guys are.

My struggles are worthless against him, he doesn't let go and keeps dragging me toward a table full of doms oww no-no-no. I try to stop, I hit him on the arm trying to get his attention but he's clearly ignoring me. "Mister please let me go" I try and say but it falls on deaf ears.

We reach the table and everyone's eyes land on me, I look down at the floor, I feel shy around new peoples and these are all alphas.

"Oww sophhhiiiiii why are you crying" I hear Rory's voice and I start sobbing in relief to hearing a familiar voice, the one holding me let go and I run to Rory and hug him. Still sobbing my eyes out till I hear another voice this one is more dominant it's laced with something dark and demands obedience.

"Little girl stop crying before you get sick," the voice says and I ignore him

"Little girl I'm talking to you now Come.Here.Now" he says and Rory gives me a little push toward the voice owner, well thank you a lot traitor.

I turn around and go toward the voice owner, the guy who has blond hair forest green eyes, and a five o'clock shadow.

He mentions to me to get closer and I shake my head no, he extends an arm toward me and gives me a little smile, hesitantly I raise my hand till it lands in his. My hand is tiny compared to his like holding a child's hand, he takes hold of my hand and pulls me toward him till I'm standing between his legs.

He gets a tissue and wipes my face and makes me blow, he then holds a water bottle against my mouth and I take a big gulp, feeling thirsty.

"Take it, easy little girl, I don't want you to get sick," he says and I slow down.

"What's your name love," he asks he got a slight accent but it's sexy as hell.

"Sophia" I whisper "Well Sophia I'm Dimitri Vitale," he says then pulls me on his lap, doesn't he knows what personal space means I try to fight and get off but his hold on me turns to steel. "Settle Sophia you want down," he asks and I nod "then first let daddy feed you"

My mouth falls open in shock and he takes the opportunity to start feeding me, I don't know what I'm eating I just chew and swallow, did he just called himself my daddy.

SIX.

After lunch, Dimitri keeps hold of my hand and no matter how much I try I can't get him to let me go. I can see Rory giggling at me and I mouth the word traitor which he laughs even more. Dimitri walks me to my class while the guy who brought me to their table in the first place the one who I learned his name is Vincent take hold of Rory's hand and it's his turn to struggle which made me giggle. Yeah, karma is a bitch.

Our next class is history but ow no not normal history, it's the history of doms and subs and how this new law made the world a better place. I take advantage of the boring class to talk to Rory.

"So you and Vincent "~Sophia "Don't start he's been trying to be my daddy since I got here" I open my mouth to ask the obvious but he beats me to it "yes I'm gay but Vincent scare me"

Oh, that does make sense Vincent is a giant compared to Rory.

"Someone catches the eye of the prince" Rory tease and I don't get it. "Dimitri he's the Vitale prince" Rory state and my mouth opens in an O shape.

For the rest of the class, I'm once again lost in my own thoughts, our last class for the day is Dom, and littles I walk into the class with Rory to see Vincent and Dimitri and another guy from their table. I take hold of Rory's hand and drag him toward the other end of the class away from Dimitri.

The teacher comes in to introduce himself as Sir Milo, he's definitely a Dom a hot one. The class is about trusting your Dom, listening to your little, trust, compromising, what to expect and what to give back.

"Okay, kids I want you pared, if your Dom is in this class go sit with them" sir milo says.

Vincent and Dimitri come toward us Vincent drag a whining Rory with him while Dimitri takes a seat next to me.

"Today's exercise is communication, talk to your partner I want you to tell me three interesting facts about him or her" ~sir milo

I turn to Dimitri he's looking at me and it makes me blush and look down, he put two fingers under my chin and raises them till our eyes meet.

"Ask away kitten" ~Dimitri "Where are you from?" ~Sophia "Russia" ~Dimitri "How long have you been a daddy Dom "~Sophia "Since I was one hundred years old" ~Dimitri "You were born a vampire?" ~Sophia "Yes kitten I was born this way" ~Dimitri "You had a little before "~Sophia "No I was never interested until ...well until you "~Dimitri "How old are you" ~Sophia I say and fight a blush "Uh-uh that's a rude question kitten" ~Dimitri

"Now it's my turn" ~Dimitri I nod and he starts asking "Siblings?" ~Sophia "Only child "~Dimitri "Parent?" ~Dimitri "Father is dead....mum....mum disowned me..." ~Sophia "its okay kitten were you always a little "~Dimitri "No, I never thought I am till I moved here" ~Sophia "Good" ~Dimitri

Our time is up and now we have to share what we found out about our partner when it's our time Dimitri went first.

"My baby is an only child who needs to be spoiled, she blushes easily and she got a big heart," Dimitri says and I blush.

Now it's my turn "uhh...he's from Russia....he was born a vampire....and he won't tell me his age" I say the last one with a pout.

After our class is over Tasha and Timmy came to get me, they said Madame P wanted to see me and Dimitri. The weird part all three of them greeted each other by saying "cousin" of course they are related.

Back at Madame P. Office, we all walk in and take a seat.

"Well Dimitri I'm glad to see someone finally got your attention," she says with a smile.

"Well, a little girl this isn't how we usually do things but well...Dimitri is kind of a special case.

Well, he....he put claims on you, so other doms won't dare to get close to you. So to avoid any problems I need to ask you if you agree to give Dimitri a chance if you say no I'll make him back off and you can meet other doms too" she says and sigh in frustration.

"She didn't even spend a full day and you already claimed her cousin you work fast" ~Timmy

They all look at me waiting for an answer, I'm still new to all this I had no idea what to do, but I knew Dimitri isn't someone to be messed with so I decided to give it a chance and I nod my head yes.

"Words kitten" ~Dimitri "Yes" ~Sophia "Yes, what?" ~Dimitri says with a raised eyebrow "Yes ....d-d-daddy" ~Sophia, damn he made me say it. "Good girl "~Dimitri

"Sophia you'll stay in your current room till the end of the week, Dimitri will walk you in and out of classes and he will talk to you about rules and punishment. Now you are all dismissed" Madame P.

I walk out still dizzy, not knowing what I got what I get myself into, was it a mistake. I have a bad headache now, I need to be alone, Dimitri is talking with his cousins I make my escape and go to my room. I have a lot to think about.

SEVEN.

I made it to my room without any problems I walk in, strip from my school uniform, and put on some PJ. I lay in bed and think, I feel tears going down my face I had no one to talk to about these things, my dad the only person who ever cared about me is dead. I cried myself to sleep.

There is banging on my door and I can hear an angry voice. I get scared and hid under the blanket hoping whoever is at the door will go away, but the banging kept going. Then it all went quiet finally, I was starting to fall back asleep when my door opened.

I hid under the blanket hoping whoever is here will leave. "What are you doing here?" came the very angry voice of Dimitri "I've been searching for you for the last three hours!!" he says and drags me off the bed he looks mad his eyes are all black, I try to pull back but he won't let me.

He takes a few deep breaths and tries to calm himself down when his eyes finally go back to their origin green, I stop fighting and look down at the floor "I'm sorry " I whisper.

He pulls close for a hug, he's all warm and I melt in his arms. "Kitten we need to go over some rules okay" ~Dimitri He made me sit on my desk, gave me a paper and pen, and made me write the rules down.

Sophia's Rules:

1- Always call me Daddy 2- Never leave or go anywhere without telling daddy first 3-Always be respectful to daddy and his friends 4- No cussing or cursing 5- Eat three meals a day 6- Don't say No to daddy, he knows best 7- Obey and Do what you're asked to do 8- No self-harming or degradation 9- Bed time is at 10 sharp 10- Ask before you eat candy and sweets 11- School work is important, do your homework and ask daddy if you need any help 12- Talk to daddy if something's wrong or you need help 13- Daddy's door is always open for you

Sophia's Punishment:

1- Time out 2- Corner time 3- Early bed time 4- No sweets 5- Privilege deprivation 6- Washing your mouth with soap 7- Spanking

When I was done writing them he asked if I have any questions or objections I said no they seem okay.

"Ok kitten let's go" ~Dimitri "Go where?" I ask when he starts dragging me out of the room

"We're going to my room so I can feed you, you missed dinner and that's against your rules" he keeps dragging me I try to stop him I'm just in my PJ.

"What is it?" he stops and looks at me I point to my PJ and he just carries me up to his hip and kept walking.

We go to another section of the castle, it's the Dom dorms. Dimitris's room well it's not a room it's a suit, he has a small kitchen a living room, a master bedroom with an adjacent room for his little and a giant bathroom with a deep tub. After the grand tour, he sits me at the breakfast bar and goes to make me a grilled cheese sandwich.

"Do u have coke?" ~Sophia "Have yes sure " ~Dimitri "Can I have some" ~Sophia "No you can have milk or juice," he says and I put my mother didn't give two damn about what I drank or ate.

I finish my sandwich with a pout for being denied a drink, after I'm done he send me to brush my teeth and get ready for bed. When I'm back he's holding a pink sippy cup I eye the cup and tell him I'm ready, he drags me toward him and sits me in his lap and hold the cup for me it got milk and vanilla, I fell asleep in his lap half way through the cup.

I wake up to kisses on my face I tried to slap whoever is kissing me away I wanted to sleep but Dimitri kept kissing me till I wake up. "Good morning little girl" god his voice is so sexy laced with sleep. "Morning" I whisper

"Up you go sweetheart it's time to get ready for school" ~Dimitri

After I get dressed in my uniform I leave my hair down not bothering with it, Dimitri lifts me and takes me to the cafeteria I don't object since it's a long walk and he's a vampire he won't get tired easily.

He set me on the same table he was sitting on yesterday I see a very happy Rory eating pancakes and some other doms that I'm not familiar with, most doms are drinking a red liquid which makes me think they are vampires. Dimitri came back with a plate of pancakes for me with some fruit salad and a sippy cup full of milk. I eat most of my food ignoring the milk.

"Someone doesn't like her milk" one of the unknown doms snitch on me

"She'll get used to it, I'm still setting her on a routine" Dimitri replies as if I'm a little girl who isn't even here.

After breakfast I try to take my backpack and leave but Dimitri won't let me, he walks me toward my first class of the day little class, he put my stuff away give me a kiss on the forehead, and tell me to be good.

I'm pissed at him, I go sit next to Rory who still got that stupid smile on his face I raise my eyebrow at him and he finally spills "Vincent is officially my daddy" he says with a big smile and a blush well I'm happy for him, he's my one and only friend around here so I give him a hug and congratulate him.

Today's class is about pacifiers, we are all required to get one, especially the little one aka me and Rory.

"If you can't afford it the school will provide you one, I want to see one on you tomorrow. Have a nice day my little angels" miss Blair dismiss us.

I and Rory both wait for our daddies to come to get us while chatting about our feeling toward pacifiers, Rory really likes the idea, I'm curious but not sure about it.

EIGHT.

My third period is PE, oww god can this get any worst. This class is a mix of subs, the coach made us run till I'm out of breath, he made us do some aerobic exercises which proved to me that I got zero muscle coordination.

But did the torture stopped there oww of course not, next the coach decided we should do a friendly game of Dodgeball!! How could that game be friendly? My muscles were burning by now and I was on the verge of fainting, I was hardly standing up until a ball hit me straight in the face, the girl who threw it made an "oww my bad " face but her eyes were gleaming with mischief she did it on purpose. I couldn't help it then I just started crying my face felt on fire.

"Below the waist Britney" the coach scream "Sorrrryyy," says Britney in a voice that shows no remorse. "I can take her to the nurse office coach"

Before I can object Britney takes hold of my hand and start dragging me out of the gym she's 5'3, her hair is box blond and her eyes are brown.

"Stay away from Dimitri he's mine you got it little girl" she growls in my face then throw me against a wall "the nurse office is that one "she nods toward a door and leave.

I go into the nurse's office, she's a middle-aged human with kind eyes, and she put ice on my face and makes sure I drink lots of water, the bell ring signaling the third period is over. The nurse tells me to stay put till the crowd dies down so I won't get hurt again. I'm still sitting there sipping my water when Dimitri came dashing in.

"Why didn't you tell me you're hurt" he practically yells at me and I flinch, his eyes are black something I'm starting to associate with his bad mood.

"You...you were in...class...I didn't know..." I stutter He turns to the nurse who looks pale as a sheet now "I'm sorry prince ... I didn't know she belongs to you...the system ....the system...didn't say she's claimed" the nurse says while she looks afraid.

I tuck on Dimitri's sleeve and he turns to me "I'm good please don't be mad" I say in a small voice, I'm a bit afraid of him too.

He gets close to me and hugs me " I went to pick you up from PE and they told me you were here baby you really scared me...next time text daddy immediately when you are hurt got it?" he says in a kind voice

"I don't have a phone," I say and look down, my mother never bought me one she said I don't deserve it.

"We'll get you one" he states, then picks me up and start walking toward the opposite side of my classes. I tuck on his sleeve again trying to get his attention "My class is the other way" I whisper I'm still too shy around him.

"You're coming with me," he says and I look at him funny "when a little get punished or sick they can stay with their daddy even in class. I have a quiz that I can't skip so you are going to be a good little girl and sit quietly with daddy got it" I nod and hide my face in his neck I'm still in my gym clothes a pair of short and a T-shirt with the school logo on it.

Dimitri walks into his class it's full of Doms, they all look at me, and I whimper and hide my face against his chest. He goes and takes a seat with me in his lap.

"She's tagging along with dom classes now" I look up and a girl Dom "She got hurt in PE so she's staying with me" ~Dimitri I look up and show her my face. "Oww your poor little thing " she rummages through her bag and retrieves a lollipop I smile and take it from her "What do you say little girl" ~Dimitri "Thank you," I say with a shy smile "God prince she's adorable" "Mine" ~Dimitri growls and the girl lift her hands in defeat

The teacher walks in and sees me sitting in Dimitri's lap "Punished or sick," he asks with a voice devoted to emotion "She got hit on the face during dodgeball" ~Dimitri

The teacher nod and start his class as if nothing happened, five minutes in and the door opens showing Andy.

"Detention Never Be Late To Class," the teacher says in his dom voice and it scares me I whimper and that get Andy attention shot towards me, I hide my face in daddy's chest till he pulls me back and looks me in the eyes.

"Can I have my candy" I whisper in his ear too afraid of his teacher he nods and I open my lollipop and stuck it in my mouth trying to stay quiet.

"Time for the quiz, little girl come to sit here with me," the teacher says and I shake my head no I want to stay with Dimitri. Instead of asking me again he looks at my daddy and he pushes me off his lap and sends me toward the teacher, I sit on his desk, they start their quiz and it's all silent I look up to see Andy giving me death glares I choke on my candy and look down.

After the quiz is over I run back to Dimitri and hide my face in his chest for the rest of the period. I hope he didn't notice my reaction to Andy, I wasn't ready to tell him anything about that topic.

NINE.

- -

After his class is over, I get to change back to my uniform and we go to lunch most of the doms coos and oohs at me for being hurt, I've had the worst and never had this many people fussing about me.

The rest of the day was peaceful I went to my classes afterward, until in Dom/little class where the teacher decided to inform all doms about the new pacifier rule. "All little should have one tomorrow, any little under the age of 4 should have one at all time" I'm starting to change my mind about sir milo.

After class Dimitri said I can go "play" with other littles, I gave him my best death glare before I went to hang out with Rory. We went to my dorm room since it's mine till the end of the week. I told Rory about Andy because well I trust him and I made him pinky promise not to tell Vincent.

We watched some Netflix well we watched Cinderella and the lion king. Until Dimitri and Vincent came and get us. Back at Dimitri's room he shows me what he got me, he got me a brand new iPhone with a unicorn cover case, his number along with Vincent, Rory, and some other "trust-worthy doms" -his words not mine- programmed in.

He also got me three new pacifiers and clips.

He tells me I can change to something comfier and we'll go have dinner, apparently, he got a full wardrobe for me here. I chose a graphic T-shirt and some jeans, daddy change to jeans and button shirt too, he eyes my outfit but says nothing. There were a lot of little girl clothes but I didn't feel like it.

Walking into the cafeteria this time I go with him to choose my food, I pick a pizza slide, fries, chocolate brownies, and Pepsi. Dimitri takes off my fries and put some vegetable instead and return my Pepsi for a sippy cup of juice. I put the Pepsi back on and he removes it we keep going back and forth till he snaps.

"If you put that thing on your tray one more time I'm taking away your desert" he threatens but I ignore him and put the Pepsi back on.

He snatches the tray away from me, takes off my Pepsi and brownie, and replaces them with juice and some strawberry-flavored yogurt.

"Hey that's not fair "I whine loudly "Don't care go sit your ass down" he says between gritted teeth.

"No no no I want my brownies back," I say and stomp my foot, well big mistake right now the whole cafeteria is looking at us.

"What did you just say to me little girl?" he says in his Dom voice

But seem like I got a death wish cause I keep my tantrum "no I want brownies" I scream

I hear the sound before I even feel the pain two loud slaps landed on my ass. "Victor sit her down please," he says to someone, that someone turns out to be one of his Dom friends he drags me to my seat, I plop down and start crying. He let me cry for a few minutes before I'm lift up and settled in his lap I don't fight him I just cry against his chest.

"Shhh shhh that's enough.....shh I didn't even pop you that hard" when I still don't stop crying he goes to dom mode again "stop crying right now or I'll give you a real reason to cry" he wipes my face although tears are still streaming down, make me drink some water before he feeds me my dinner I fight him the whole time not wanting to eat.

I ended up sitting in his lap with my hand crossed on my chest still sniffling while he drank his blood. He took me back toward his dorm and took me straight toward the bathroom. He started filling the tub while I'm still ignoring him, he put some bubble bath in the tub and it's starting to call my name. He comes to undress me and I fight again, I don't want him seeing me naked.

"Sophia I'm your Dom and your daddy. I will see you naked so no use to fight unless you want a real spanking" he growls at me.

He's right so I let him undress me and put me in the bath it was amazing until he got a washcloth and started washing me, after I squirmed around too much he said in a calm voice " baby girl I'm going to wash you every night before bed so please stop fighting me and enjoy "

I'm a submissive at heart, his dom voice, well his dom voice can make me do anything he asks for so I do relax after my bath he dress in PJ and get one of my new pacifiers.

"Come on let's try it" when I shake my head no he says "you want to try it tomorrow in class alone or now with me here"

Well, he did make a point so I open my mouth I spit it out immediately "I don't like it" I pout.

"Kitten give it a minute " he pleads with me and stuck it back in my mouth I start sucking on it, his movement helping me relax, I fell asleep with a paci.

TEN.

Today's Friday, I'm in my school uniform but a pacifier clipped on my shirt. I tried to compromise and put it in my bag but daddy wouldn't let me. I pout the whole way toward the cafeteria, he goes to get me my breakfast and I don't even bother to go along with him I stomp to our table and see that Rory too got a paci clipped to his shirt, well at least I'm not alone.

Today's class is about regression, how to go into our little space, what can trigger it, and what can snap us out. The last five minutes were spent with paci inside our mouths. My academic classes passed quickly thank god I didn't have English today, so most of them were with Rory. In our last class with our daddies, we had to sit in their lap the whole period while Sir Milo explained about trust and caregiving while in little space.

After the class was over Tasha and Timmy came to get us to Madame P's office, I had to make my decision if I want Dimitri to be my daddy or not. Well the answer was simple I said yes, I had to sign a few papers that made me officially his, and I got a new school Id with my name on it "Sophia Vitale"

I moved well officially moved to Dimitri's room, we spent Saturday talking and getting to know each other. I found out why they all call him prince due to his status with the mafia he's the Vitale empire heir. I still wasn't cool with the criminal part but I could do nothing about it. We watched movies he let me chose what I want to watch, he cooked for me instead of going to the cafeteria, we even colored together he got me so many crayons, water paint, coloring books. I got more used to my pacifier, I haven't slipped to a full little mindset yet but I was close.

The weekend passed quietly for us, Monday I had a new schedule, daddy's doing of course. Instead of PE, I got "little activities" and I got a new class of English along with an extra course about vampires. Mine and Rory's schedule are identical now so that's a plus, in every class, I would see one of Dimitri doms friend they are Victor, Dante, and Maria the girl who gave me candy. If not them then I got Vincent or daddy along with me. I was never alone which made me feel kind of safe.

As the days went by I was getting used to my routine, waking up with daddy getting ready for school, breakfast, classes, lunch, classes, homework, quality time with daddy, dinner, bath, and finally bed.

Its Thursday morning when daddy breaks the news to me "Sophia love I have some work to do, I won't be at the school today but I'll be back by dinner time. Be a good girl for me okay" I feel my eyes start watering I don't want him to leave.

"No don't go," I say and the tears start falling. "Baby baby come on don't cry, please. Maria, Victor, and Dante will walk you and Rory to and from class they'll take care of you till I'm back okay" he says and kisses my forehead I'm still crying I don't want him to leave. He gets up and lifts me on his hip to go get some breakfast I cling to him like a koala refusing to be put down. I eat a few bites of my breakfast while sitting on his lap, he takes me toward my first class and I start crying again not wanting him to leave.

"Shh that's enough kitten stop crying....I'll be back by dinner time and I better hear that you've been a good girl or there would be consequences" he stuck my pacifier into my mouth and go talk to my teacher.

I'm grumpy all day I don't participate in class, I don't eat lunch no matter how much the other three try to feed me. By time for our last period I'm really pissed I have no daddy to sit with me. The moment I walk into class with red puffy eyes and pout on my face Sir Milo calls me to him.

"What's got you so mad little girl," he asks "Daddy's busy" I grumble "Oww come on sweetheart I'm sure he got some important errands to run" he kisses my forehead and stuck my paci in my mouth I spit it out immediately. He gives me a stern look and sends me to my seat.

I don't pay attention in class and Sir Milo calls me on it twice, by the third time he got enough from me and send me to stand in the corner. I stayed in the corner for a full fifteen minutes. When the bell rings I try to run out of class but he calls me back in

"If your Dom isn't here that doesn't give you a free pass to sulk and not pay attention in class. Dimitri will be notified about your behavior you are dismissed" great now my teacher is threatening to snitch on me.

I stay inside our dorm till dinner I try to skip but victor said I either go with him or he's calling Dimitri what is it with these people threatening to call my daddy.

I'm wearing one of Dimitris hoodie with some legging, Victor asks me to bring a paci when I gave him sass about not needing one he reminded me that's it's a school rule since my regression age is below four. I stomp back inside and snatch one in my hand and walk back out. Victor holds his hand palm up waiting for me to give it to him, when I do he clip it to my hoodie. He tries to carry me but I refuse to choose to walk....a very bad choice indeed.

ELEVEN.

I decided to walk toward the cafeteria, one of my worst choices ever. I'm walking and paying zero attention to who's there, walking with Dimitri means people move out of our way but now I'm alone.

Well that about to change soon when someone slams me against a wall

"What do we have here a little slut" I look up to see Andy and Britney together this can't be good.

"The prince got tired of your dirty pussy and sent you away," he says and laughs

"You think you're untouchable now huh" he slams my small body against the wall and it hurt "all-mighty hiding behind the most powerful doms NOBODY LOVE A CRYBABY" he punches me in the stomach " stay out of my way bitch "

I'm crying now and Britney comes closer she plays with my paci teasing me with it and laughing about what a crybaby I am when she does push my pacifier against my mouth Andy snatch it off and throw it on the floor.

"Let's go sir you don't want to spend time on this loser," Britney says pulling my tormentor away.

I sit on the floor and cry, I thought I got rid of him and his bullying days. But was he right does Dimitri hate me is that why he left me here alone. I keep crying till I feel a hand on my shoulder its Tasha she's looking at me with pity in her eye, Tasha bends down and lifts me off the ground then starts walking toward the cafeteria.

They all ask me what happened and I just shake my head no, if I tell he'll probably kill me.

"Sophia where's your pacifier" victor asks with a raised eyebrow he thinks I took it off. I shrug and mumble it fall.

They won't let me go back to the dorm and I cried so hard I ended up vomiting, I hadn't eaten anything that day so it was mostly stomach fluid that burned my throat going out.

"I'll take her to the nurse the poor baby" ~Tasha

I shake my head vigorously no, I just vomited on the floor of the cafeteria, all I want is to be left alone until I feel strong familiar arms around me, they lift off my seat and pull me against a powerful chest. Daddy's back.

I clung to him and cry, I missed him so much, the next thing I know we are in our dorms in the bathroom he's washing my face with some warm water. He skip my daily bath and change me into a footie onesie, I felt all warm in it. He's doing something in the kitchen but my head is against his chest and I don't bother looking. He sat on the sofa with me cradled against his chest like a small baby, he got a bottle! A milk bottle against my lips. I keep my mouth shut but he won't take no for an answer he teases the bottle nipple against my lips till I give up and open my mouth. The milk is warm and has a hint of vanilla I drink the whole thing falling asleep in daddy's arm.

The next morning it's Friday, I don't want to go to school I try to whine and tell my daddy I'm sick but he doesn't buy it and still gets me out of bed and dressed. I didn't do my homework yesterday when I tell my daddy so he's furious at me.

"I got reports that you've been a brat all day. And now you tell me you didn't do your homework! I'm very disappointed in you Sophia" he scolds me and I cry but instead of being babied and cooed, I'm dragged to our breakfast bar he sits me down and makes me do my homework while eating breakfast.

We're late for my first period when we got in he just talk to my teacher telling her I was a naughty girl in front of the whole class and they all laugh at me. He tells me to behave and leave, I'm cranky most days since I didn't even want to be here and the other littles are making fun of me.

One particular brat that's in my first period and the third which instead of PE is little activities now, the class is about playing and running on a playground. It got seven kids including me and Rory, all below the age of four. So this brat Juliana has been pushing my buttons all day, she calls me a crybaby, a brat, and today's new nickname thanks to daddy naughty.

Rory was pushing me on the swings, we take a turn pushing each other cause it's more fun. So this brat comes over and tells me to get off the swings.

"No uh it's her turn" ~Rory "She's a brat and a naughty girl she doesn't get a turn "~Juliana

When we both ignored her she pushes Rory to the ground, nobody pushes my friend, and I know she keeps picking on him. I might not be able to face my own bully but this girl is 5'3 and a little, I think I can take her.

I jump from the swing and push her back, she gets off and slaps my face that bitch I jump on her and start beating her, Rory gets in the middle trying to separate us. Well, the keyword is trying cause we don't stop till the teacher gets there and we are all sent to Madame P's office.

TWELVE.

✱ Dimitri POV

I was feeling terrible about yesterday I had to go and take care of some business, I've been delaying this errand since I didn't want to leave my princess alone. Well till my father called and tore me a new asshole for delaying family business.

I had three of my most trusted friends and they are part of the family to keep an eye on her. All I got all day were reports about her giving them hard time. When I got a message from Sir Milo saying he had to put her in the corner I was seeing red, she's getting it when I'm back. On my way back I asked if she ate, it's in her rules to eat three times a day and god knows she can't afford to skip a meal she's so skinny. When they told me she didn't make it to dinner yet I sent victor to drag her ass, Victor is six feet tall who's made of muscle and a no-nonsense vibe he's a dom that doesn't take no for an answer.

When I made it to school I went straight to the cafeteria to see my baby vomiting, she cried till she got sick which is a habit of hers, she told me she did it all the time back home. How she didn't know she's a little is above me, she's a big crybaby but she's my crybaby and I love everything about her.

I knew she studied about bottles in her little class, doms get reports about everything their baby learns, it wasn't mandatory for her to try it till next week so I took my chance and gave her one, she took it like a champ and even fell asleep after drinking it.

She tried to skip school this morning and when I didn't let her she confessed she didn't do her homework, if I learned something yesterday then it's my baby isn't ready to be left alone, I'll have to find a new game plan for next time I need to run some family errands.

My schedule consists of mostly DDLG classes with few advanced academic ones, I did shuffle my schedule a bit to get the same classes as my baby.

Right now I'm sitting in a boring advanced calculus class when Timmy knocks on the door. Timy says Madame P. is asking for me and Vincent to her office.

Timy and Tasha are twins and my cousins, they work at the school as "counselor" code name to spy for my father.

When they find a sub with potentials they alarm the family, I knew about Sophia the minute they went to get her. The first time I saw her crying and then calming down in my arms I knew she was mine.

"Got any idea what's this about," Vincent asks me and I shake my head no.

Well, I wouldn't in a million years imagine the scenario we found in Madame P.'s office. Standing in front of her are three rough-looking littles, they all have a guilty look on their face, I share a quick chuckle with Vincent before I put my poker face on. If Sophia sees that I'm smiling she'll think she can get off the hook but little does she knows her first punishment is coming soon.

The last person that I wanted to see enter the room after us. Damien Stewart belongs to a little gang. They think they are the kings of the street, well they aren't. We've been at each other necks since our first day at this school five years ago.

Our littles fought with his brat, the teacher had to separate them when they got physical.

"Take your littles, punish them as you see fit, plus they'll spend the rest of the day with you.

And I must point to that Sophia and Juliana were the ones fighting while Rory was trying to get between them." ~Madame P.

Well, poor Rory, he should have called a teacher, he's not getting off the hook easily. Vincent is the strictest daddy I know and although Rory is very well behaved him get into trouble often. As for my little fighter, who's tearing up, she's going to get it.

We all carry our littles and leave the office until Damien talked of course "Keep your little brat away from mine" he sneers and leaves.

I take my girl to our dorm and set her on her feet she tries to run away but I keep hold of her hand. "You got thirty seconds to explain" ~Dimitri "She pushed Rory and then pushed me and hit me" ~Sophia "And you thought it was okay to hit her back instead of calling a teacher or calling me" ~Dimitri "You weren't there" she pouts "You can always call me and I'll come or tell your teacher you need me or just tell her about the other little " I scold her she keep silent so I continue "fighting isn't acceptable now come here"

I drag her toward me while she cries, I put her on my lap facing down, lift her skirt and smack her pretty bum.

"Count them," I say but she doesn't comply

Smack smack "Count them or I'll just keep going till you do" I threaten

Smack "o...o-one" she starts good

I give her ten smacks on her bum and make her stand in the corner for another 5 minutes.

"Come here" I wipe her face from tears and tell her how much I love her. She calms down without any problems, I get her a water bottle and carry her toward my next class.

I go to sit down with her on my lap she wiggles a little to find a comfy position with her red bum, she doesn't tolerate pain, even though they were like fifteen smack in total, they hurt.

I look at Vincent seat but he's not here yet, the first bell ring, we're five minutes into class and he finally shows up with a crying Rory.

Our teacher isn't kind on people who are late, it's why Vincent didn't want to take dom/subclass with him, to begin with but after we shuffled our schedules to match our littles he ended up stuck here with me.

THIRTEEN.

The teacher raised an eyebrow at Vincent he didn't even bother talking and we can all feel his alpha aura.

"Sorry I'm late but someone won't stop crying," Vincent says while still rubbing Rory's back to calm him down.

"Punished or sick?" Sir ask "Punished" Vincent reply he just nods and then looks at me "punished," I say knowing he wants to know.

"Boys a word" well that's weird I get up with Sophia still cradled in my arms.

"Today's class about sub punishment aftercare, you mind if we take yours as a case study," he asks.

I look at Vincent and he looks lost, this is the class we learn about how to take care of our subs, we know aftercare is important, well if it helps Rory stop his crying I'm in.

"We don't mind sir," I say for both of us.

"Today we are going to talk about post punishment care, if you punish your sub how can you make them stop crying or not afraid of you or not to hate you.

Since we got two littles with us, we're going to take them as case studies"
~teacher

Sophia hides her face in my chest while Rory, Rory haven't stopped crying
or clutching Vincent neck since they came, what the hell did Vincent do
to him.

"Why do you think one of them is crying while the other isn't" ~teacher

"She didn't get punished and he did" "He took it easy on her" "The boy is
a brat"

"Well let's ask them who got punished and who didn't" the teacher look at
us, I knew we had to answer him since we agreed to this.

"She got a spanking" ~Dimitri "I scolded him no spanking" ~Vincent

"Okay so take us to a new point, verbal punishment can be as bad or worse
than physical ones. And they both require post-care.

Ideas to why he's still crying" ~teacher

"He was mean to him" "He broke his heart the meanie" "Called him a bad
name"

The teacher looks at Vincent, he didn't like what he heard, he might be
strict but he really loves his little Rory.

"I yelled at him for putting himself between two fighting littles instead of
calling the teacher or calling me. I was disappointed in him because he
knows better. He got a few scratches on him and the girls pulled his hair"
~Vincent

"Class now you know the reason how would you solve this problem"
~teacher

"Stuck a pacifier in, it's like a mute button" "Let him cry it out" "Tell him to stop crying" "Put him in a corner till he stops" "Bribery"

"Rory is scared of the yelling maybe try talking calmly to him, he loves his daddy very much and he did say he was disappointed in him," Maria says

Thank God we have Maria in class with us, she's a mommy Dom and familiar with Rory and Vincent relation.

"Bribery is off the table you aren't supposed to award a misbehaving sub, it defies the punishment and guys grow a heart before you adopt a little. What Maria said is the most true.

Vincent talks to him, calmly. If the Dom is calm the sub will calm down too, if the Dom is angry he'll get scared of being punished again."

Vincent whisper something in Rory's ear and finally, he stops crying, he gets up and starts walking in the back of the class with Rory in his arm it takes him about three minutes till Rory fall asleep. The whole class was silent just watching them.

"Communication is the key, don't be afraid to apologize if you went too hard. Tell your sub you love them, calm them down. Now let's move to the physical aspect of post-care"

The rest of the class pass quickly, Sophia was awake the whole time, it looks like the class fascinated her. Lunch passed without Rory or Vincent since he took him back to the dorm, we were walking toward my next period with her holding my hand.

My next class is a vampire class the second we make it to class she went and hid behind my back. I was the only blue tie there, the others were looking at her funny, we all go to the same school but that doesn't mean we intervene with everyone or every category.

I take my seat and pull her to my lap she's whimpering and on the edge of tears, if I miss this class my father would be notified, this class is kind of important. So I get close and whisper in her ear "kitten there's nothing to be afraid of, I'm here and if you be my good girl I'll let you chose your dessert for tonight" I try the bribery method, I don't let her eat much sugar before bed, I want her to be healthy, not high on sugar. She nods and hides her face in my chest, I pop her paci in her mouth maybe she'll sleep for the rest of the class.

When our teacher comes in the eye her funny, again me being the only daddy in this class means we never have a little tagging along, well till now.

This class is all about our powers, when vampires reach a certain age they get some powers most known are reading the minds, controlling small emotions, hypnotism, some can lift a light object off the ground or control the electricity. It all depends on how strong you are, the class also talks about feeding on human donors how to make them forget it even happened. Sophia had a death grip on my shirt the whole time with her eyes shut close, I don't think she like this class at all, when we walk out she let out a long breath.

Sir Milo's class was about bottle feeding, and how it helps to regress, Sophia was silent the whole class, I haven't forgotten that she got corner time yesterday and plans on talking about it with her later.

FOURTEEN.

Vincent POV

I've started coming to this school when my best friend Dimitri did, his father in the don of our family while mine is his right hand, the underboss. We aren't related by blood but we are all a family, when we got classified we both knew we were going to be doms, but being daddy dom was kind of a shocker, I didn't even know we had a soft side.

No little catches our interest, we did mess around with other subs but no one special. Well until Rory came in, he was such a cute little thing. I saw him for the first time in sir Milo's class, one of the other little was bugging him so I stepped in. For the first week, he kept trying to avoid me or run away every time I get close to him.

I told Madame P. that I wanted him and so did two other doms, when he was asked who he wanted he cried and ran out scared. I used everything I had to convince Madame P. to let him be mine, I begged, I threatened, I tried to bribe her and I even shed a few tears till she said yes. We all talked and he agreed to be my nonofficial baby, for the next week he was mine. The week afterward came Sophia and they became friends, somehow seeing

Sophia and knowing she's going to be Dimitri's baby girl made him agree to finally be officially mine.

We finished our first semester in school, since we take classes all year long we finished the summer semester and started the fall one.

Its Halloween the best holiday of all, and this year I have a little to dress and play with, I dress Rory in sweat pants and a hoodie that says "property of daddy"

And his converse something to keep him warm but also easy to change to so he can try on his costume.

We met with Dimitri and Sophia who's also dressed in sweats, we all head toward the custom store. I give Rory the don't leave my hand talk and head inside, it's packed since all subs get to wear costumes. Most doms just wear jeans and a shirt, not bothering.

Sophia chose a blue Cinderella costume, of course, she wanna be a princess while my Rory is being picky, he refused every outfit I have chosen for him stating he wanted to be scary and not cute. After much more debating and searching, we decide on a devil costume which made him look adorable but I wouldn't break his heart and tell him that.

The next day I dress my baby in black pants, a black sweater put on his red plastic horn, tail and wings cause why not, and gave him his pitchfork, Maria came by and added a bit of makeup to make him look "scary" -still adorable in my eyes- and we were good for the day.

The little didn't have any classes today, they get to go over the doms classes for trick or treating. I didn't see Rory today yet, they won't come to our class till the fourth period.

Finally when the fourth period came so did my little boy, he ran straight to me he looked a bit pale. "You okay baby boy," I ask while petting his hair. "Daddy my stomach hurt," Rory says in his little voice, he slipped a couple of times so far, whenever he gets in trouble or scared. I lift his head and check his forehead his a little warm to touch and he's clutching his stomach.

"Rory how much candy did you have," I ask in my daddy's voice he squirm and try to get away from me but I won't let him. "Little boy I asked you a question"

He lifts both his hand and shows me all his fingers, He Ate How Much Candy. My eyes widen with shock no wonder his stomach hurt, I never allow him more than one candy a day.

I take his hand drag him with me toward Dimitri who's fussing over his little princess "Princess how much candies did you ate, "I ask her She raises three fingers "daddy said only thee before dinner"

Well at least one of us thought about setting limits. "What's wrong Vin" ~Dimitri "Rory ate too much candy, I'm taking him to the nurse. I was just checking that Sophia doesn't have a stomach ache too" I inform and he nods, Sophia and Rory are now family to us and we take care of family.

I drag him to the nurse's office after she checks on him she suggested I give him some laxative and feed him bland food for the rest of the day. We spent half the lunchtime in the bathroom with Rory crying and whining, the other half me trying to feed him lunch.

He asked to go back with his friend but I refused he was a bad boy, he knew better than to eat that much candy. My next class was with Victor, I tried to sit Rory in my lap but he kept squirming off, so I popped him on the thighs.

"Daddy can I sit alone," he asked me with tears in his eyes, I know he wants to be with his friends. So I compromised and put him on an empty desk between me and Victor.

Our teacher was Mistress Angela, although she was anything but an angel.

"Ow I didn't know I had Lucifer in my class" she purred at Rory and he paled "who do you belong to little devil, I might just keep you for myself" she pops his nose and he side hugs my arm.

He did ask to sit alone so it serves him right, halfway through the class Rory got up and sat in Victor's lap! Victor, not mine. He isn't even a daddy Dom, I can feel my eyes goes dark, vampires are supper possessive and that little boy belongs to me.

"Excuse me Mistress," I say to our teacher and she nods.

I get up from my seat, take hold of Rory arm I pull him with too much force off victor's lap land two smack on his ass, and drag him to sit on my lap with my arms possessively around him, he whimpers and squirms but I don't let him go. He starts crying so I stuck his paci on again with too much force and growl "mine".

"I do love a bit of jealousy" mistress Angela says and laugh her signature dark laugh

FIFTEEN.

R ory POV

I was sceptical at first about having Vincent as my daddy he's nice to me and all, but he's also very strict and I wasn't sure if I want to go through it or not, to have him to be my official daddy, the one in charge. I knew I wouldn't find a better daddy or one that I would like as much as him, and when I saw Sophia join the family and how well the whole family treated her and me, I wanted to make it official.

I'm a good little, or at least I try my best to be one, and I'm grateful for everything Vincent gave me, before him, I lived in the orphanage and that wasn't any fun, wasn't fun at all, it was hell on earth. I got abused all the time by the worker and bigger kids, and anyone else who was bigger in me in both size and age. When I was sixteen, which took a very long time, a whole sixteen years to reach the big age of sixteen, the one where I can get away from this place, I was officially an adult in their eyes, I ran toward the classification centre hoping they'll take me anywhere away from that hell hole. I went through the classification like everyone else and that's how I ended up here, they picked me up from the centre and brought me over, and now that's all history.

I probably shouldn't have eaten that much candy, daddy Vincent never allow me more than one which is very little in candy counting, and back at the orphanage, I was allowed none which is worse! So after seeing that many candies I couldn't resist I ate way too many, I ate until my little heart was satisfied.

When we got to my daddy class my stomach was killing me, I couldn't hide the pain and I felt myself slip into little me. Daddy scolded me for all the candy I ate and made me take an icky-tasting medicine that made me poop. He took me to class with him for the rest of the day, since he wouldn't let me go back to my friends I didn't want to sit with him.

If I knew who the teacher was I would've stayed with him, she scares the shit out of me, and when I hugged his arm he wouldn't even hug back, that's cold from him. So I turned to Victor who held my hand, when the evil teacher kept looking at me I got up and sat in Victor's lap. He was surprised at first but let me stay there, he's part of the family, and my friend, and I'm a little it's okay to sit with your friend and uncle.

Until daddy's voice came "Excuse me Mistress" I thought he was going to leave the class and leave me here to fend for myself. But instead of leaving, he yanked me off Victor's lap popped me twice on the bum and put me in his lap his hand was like steel and he was leaving bruises on me. I felt my eyes tear up, he was hurting me, when I groaned and tried to get out of his arms, he stuffs my paci into my mouth with force and growled mine.

I cried in silence for the rest of the class about why he was being this mean to me. Our last class was with Sir Milo, most littles were back with their daddies and mommies. They were all happy except for me, I was afraid and in pain. Vincent wouldn't let me sit alone and I was pouting the whole time.

After class, he took me to our room and stripped me from my costume when he saw the bruises he left on me and paled "ow shit baby".

He kissed my bruises, and my face and apologized to me, he knew what happened to me at the orphanage so he felt extra guilty. A few kisses landed on my mouth and I kissed back, it was my first real kiss. He took it slowly first, letting me get used to it and lean into the kiss, when I opened my mouth he invaded it with his tongue.

I was blushing like a tomato when he pulled back, "How about a bottle and a nap I'm sorry I hurt you, baby boy."

"I kiss Love kiss you kiss Very kiss Very kiss Much kiss"

He cuddled with me and gave me my bottle then spooned me and we both took a nap. After my nap, we had dinner mostly bland for me and no candy.

But I was okay with it, I think I'm falling in love with my daddy.

SIXTEEN.

S ophia POV

I've been here for a couple of months, I'm actually enjoying my time here. Daddy Dimitri get me anything I want and take good care of me, I love every moment well except waking up early.

"Come on princess it's waking up time" ~Dimitri I growl and hide my face in the pillow, we sleep in the same bed we did that since my first night here, he doesn't touch me sexually although I know one day he will.

"Come on kitten up you go, need help getting ready," he says and lifts off the bed. "No daddy I'm a big girl " I reply and go get ready, I put on my skirt, long sleeve white shirt, and a light sweater with the school logo on it. It's our winter version of the uniform.

I come outside of the bedroom to see him drinking a cup of blood-laced coffee, he eyes my clothes and raises a brow. I just shrug and go get my backpack, I'm marching toward the door when he takes hold of the back of my sweater and drags me back toward our room.

"Hey hey let me go let me go" I try and fight. "Settle little girl, it's cold and you need something under your skirt" ~Dimitri he tried to put some leggings on me but I fight not wanting them and screaming nu nu nu.

"Sophia not up for discussion stop your tantrum," he says and manages to put them on me. He drags me to breakfast pouting and wearing leggings.

"Why the frown pretty girl" victor asks me and I just shrug. Rory comes in all wrapped up in his sweater and an extra hoodie that looks too big on him and a beanie I couldn't help but laugh.

"Vincent how is he supposed to breathe?" Maria asks with a laugh.

"You do know he can get sick from a heat stroke" ~Dante

He's the quietest one of the group, don't takes off Rory beanie and jacket and kiss the little guy on the head. And here I am whining about leggings.

I and Rory spend most of our first-class talking and paying no attention to our teacher Miss Blair. We had a pop quiz by the end of the period oww shit. Plz, be MCQ plz be MCQ. But of course, with my luck it wasn't, I butchered the quiz and not in a good way. After the class, Miss Blair asked me and Rory to wait and talk to her.

She gave us the graded quiz we both had an F. Oww I'm dead. "I want both your daddies to sign them by tomorrow morning"

I look at Rory as we walk to our next class " how we going to show it to them?" he asks me "I don't know maybe we don't show them it and she'll forget about it" I suggest.

By dinner time we couldn't come up with a better plan may be forging their signature, asking another Dom to sign them but none of them would work so we went with the first one.

I was the perfect angel for the rest of the evening and even the next morning, I let him dress me in tights under my skirt and ate breakfast without any complaints.

My first class passer and Miss Blair didn't even ask about our quizzes it looks like our plan worked that until Miss Blair stop us again after class.

"I need to see the signature of your doms guys," she says and we look at each other

"Uhm...miss bee...our Dom didn't sign the quiz" ~Sophia "And why's that?" ~Blair "Uh...uhh...we forgot" I blur "Go stand in the corner both of you" ~Blair says in a dominant voice that we never heard before.

We stood in the corner for about five minutes before we heard murmurs behind us, followed by Miss Blair voice come over.

We go over and face two very pissed-off doms their eyes are dark and scary. I feel myself slip to my younger age space, it's the first time I fully slip and it has to be when I'm in trouble.

Vincent take hold of Rory arm and growl "did you lie to me, little boy"

I knew it was my fault and not Rory, I don't want him to get in trouble "Uncle Vincent, it was my idea not Rory please don't be mad at him" I say.

Uncle Vincent take Rory by hand and walk him away while daddy takes mine and dragged me to the other side of the class. "Why did you lie kitten?"~Dimitri "Cause you would yell at me," I say and start crying "And lying tone is acceptable," he ask and I shake my head no "I'm not going to spank you, you're getting grounded that means no TV, no playtime, no dessert, and an early bedtime. Am I clear" ~Dimitri

I nod my head while tears are still streaming down my face. He sends me to my next class instead of taking me with him to his, while Rory go with his daddy to class. My next class is littles activity the same brat Juliana tries to pick on me, she pulls my hair and pushes me to the ground. Instead of fighting her, I go tell the teacher.

I'm in my full little space, I've been like this since daddy yelled at me. I tell my teacher what happened and Juliana got corner time while she tells me to go and play. I don't want to play I sit down on the floor and sob quietly.

SEVENTEEN.

W hen the bell rings all the little leaves the playground while I stay on the floor until I see a shadow towering over me, I look up and see Timmy.

"What are you doing here little girl" ~Timmy "The meanie girl pulled my hair and pushed me," I say with a pout "Did you tell your teacher" ~Timmy I nod and tell him she got corner time

"Then why is the little girl crying" he asks and scoops me up "I want daddy" I pout "Oww baby girl daddy is in class" he tires reasoning with me but I'm in full little space I don't understand why I can't go to my daddy. My next class is math and I wasn't ready to sit in class and be a big girl. Timy is walking me toward my math class and I start crying and trashing I didn't want to go in.

"That's enough what's wrong with you," Timmy says in a dominant voice "I want....d-ddd-daddy," I say between sobs. Timy walks to the other side of the building where I know my daddy is. He knocks on the door and opens it I see daddy sitting and I squirm out of Timmy hands and go run to him.

"Baby girl slows down what are you doing here," he asks me.

Isn't he happy to see me, I missed him, I start tearing up.

"I'm sorry sir, I'll take care of her," daddy says to the teacher and lift me to his lap "kitten what happened," he asks and I tell him about everything, the meanie Juliana, the teacher, and how I missed him so Timmy brought me here. "Kitten how old are you," he asks and I lift two fingers. He smiles a big smile and gives me a hug. Oww, he did miss me yey.

I look at his teacher I know him from our first semester everyone calls him sir so I never knew his name.

"Littles can be super vulnerable when in little space. They need your attention and care, but if let's say you're in class or a business meeting how do you make your little busy without breaking their heart"

"Give them candy," one guy says "For the million-time Jeff you can't bribe your little with candy all the time, they'll end up with bad teeth. Other suggestions" ~sir "Give them a toy or something to play with," a girl says.

"That's a good idea why don't you try it El?" "Try it sir" the El girl reply

"Yes we have a little right here, give her something to do" ~sir

The girl gets up and walk toward us, she squats so she's on the same eye level as me "hey little girl I'm Ellie , I have a pencil case full of crayons how about you and me color your daddy a pretty picture" I look up at daddy and he nods so I go with her.

I sit on my own desk and she gives me the pencils and white paper.

"Great job El, never be frustrated with your little, a good daddy or mommy need to always stay calm. If you need to work fine something for your little to do. Now today's topic is a diaper and pull-ups. Do all little needs them ...." sir says and I stop paying attention to him too busy drawing.

I gave my daddy the drawing after class and he really loved it, I spent the rest of the day in little space and went to all of Daddy's classes. I didn't get any candy or TV time and I was put to bed early but it was okay since I was exhausted, being a little is hard work.

I was in and out of little space the whole week, sometimes I'll go to class others daddy will come to mine or I'll go to his. It was getting really cold outside so stopped complaining about tights and sweaters.

It's the weekend daddy's taking me to town with him, he says he got a few errands to run and if I'm good he'll buy me a toy. We go to the warehouse where daddy and other guys talk in a different language I saw uncle victor, Dante there. He set me in his office and gave me my coloring books, I was taken by the colors until I hear my voice being called I look up and see Rory with Uncle Vincent I run and give Rory a hug. He's in his little space too so we both color and watches TV till it's time to go to the TOY STORE.

I got a new stuffy it's a blue elephant, I got a few Barbie's, and a kitchen set, and even a truck. Daddy got me new pacies since I use those daily. I was the luckiest little ever.

EIGHTEEN.

Days came and go, it was different than my old life, I was never alone I had the best daddy ever with me, I had my friend Rory and my uncles and Aunt Maria, the whole school was a great new experience, I was happy most days. I had a new schedule in school mostly little classes with my daddy and other doms, they kept saying I'm almost ready, and they'd drop a hint here and there about what a big girl I'm, although I'm just a little, but I was doing great, and I'm almost ready, I had no idea what I was ready for but apparently, I'm almost there.

Today I have a physical examination, I don't think I was meant to know about that, but I heard daddy talking on the phone and taking an appointment for me, I was healthy, what the examination is for? I wasn't looking forward to it, I don't like doctors, I don't enjoy anyone but daddy touching me anywhere. Daddy dresses me in a pink sweater with overalls and jeans this morning, he then put my hair in a bun and put my socks and shoes on, I'm a princess and I don't have to do anything, including dressing up. He drags me to the clinic, I didn't want to go, nor walk over there, we're still in the academy, and yes we have a full clinic at school other than the nurse's office who would've known.

The doctor takes my height and weight I finally hit the one-hundred pounds and I'm finally considered healthy, I'm no longer underweight. He checks my body I got no bruises or cuts, daddy never hit or spank hard enough to bruise which I'm grateful for. He tries to take some blood, well try because I kept crying and fighting too afraid of needles.

Daddy pinned me down while the doctor took some blood and then injected some stuff in me, I had no idea what was happening.

After crying myself to sleep I woke up in our bedroom with me cradled against Dimitri.

"Can I talk to big Sophie please?" he asks and I nod trying to wake up and be big me?

"We need to have a talk sweetheart, you want some coffee?" I shake my head no I hate coffee "want Pepsi?" I nod yes, I have no idea why he's trying to put caffeine in me but I'm not going to complain. He keeps a hand on the Pepsi can so it won't fall from me.

"Okay baby, your blood results just came in," he says oww maybe I'm sick?

"Your blood is compatible, I want you to be changed, the doctor assured me it's safe and you'll survive. You'll be changed in a few days" he says matter of facts as if I had no say about it, well I don't but he could try and make it sound a little softer.

I let go of the Pepsi can, a good thing he's holding it with me. I go out running, I don't know where I'm going but I need time to process what just happened, I reach the garden and sit outside to think.

He just informed me I'm going to be changed to a vampire!! The law is actually with him, not me, he's my Dom and he's a vampire which gives him the upper hand in our relationship.

If he wants to change me to a vampire there is nothing I could do about it, some wait till their sub is a little older but he wants me to stay sixteen. I won't age above sixteen, my skin will be flawless my eye vision would be perfect, I'll look like a porcelain doll. A doll that would never grow up, he wanted a baby that never grew up and he'll get one.

I could still have children I learned that in my classes, they'll grow like a normal human but would never look a day older than twenty-five. Just like their father while I'll always be the same, the change is done in a hospital I'll be sedated and will feel nothing but when I wake up it will take me time to be able to control my body and muscles, I'll be a baby dependent on him.

Again I was lost in my thoughts, I didn't even notice the presence with me, it was Andy and he looked pissed more than usual.

"I heard rumours that the prince is changing you" he spit the words in my face as if they are the most disgusting thing ever.

"But well you're lucky someone promised me lots of good things in exchange for delivering you to him," he says the last words and sprays something in my face, and everything goes dark.

NINETEEN.

D imitri POV

After Sophia's blood test today I was informed it's safe for her to be changed, I love everything about her, her small nose, her little body, the pink lips. She was just adorable, she slipped more and more into her little headspace, she'll sleep with her blue elephant stuffy that she named Dumbo, she'll spend hours playing with her toys or coloring. But the best part ever was when she called me daddy and run toward or hide her face in my chest, even when she was in trouble and would bite her lips and tear up.

I loved her, yes I fucking adored her, whether she was big or small I fell in love head over heels with her. My job isn't the safest job ever and people who are important to me can get killed or hurt, everyone in school knew she's my little now which put her in great danger.

I wanted to wait for a little till she's eighteen but I was receiving threats all about her, our family enemies wanted to hurt her. I'm three hundred years old, most vampire get their sub or little when they're about one hundred. I went to other schools, I went to auctions and little events but I could never find a little that's perfect for me before her.

Five years ago my father decided to make me and Vincent attend this school in the hope we'll find a little and we'll learn a bit more about being vampires, it was also good publicity for me, for people to see me and know I'm not someone to mess with.

I wanted to spare her the fear of being threatened, so I just informed her that she's getting changed, her reaction was better than I thought. I gave her fifteen minutes before I went to search for her.

I searched most of the school and still couldn't find her, I called in for help. After a full hour of searching and still not finding her, my mood was going from dark to darker. She did not just run away from me , I don't care if I have to force her to be my baby , SHE'S MINE.

Another hour went by before my phone ringed "Yes" "We got the girl, you want her vitale, and maybe I'll send her back... Peace by peace"

The line went dead, but I knew the owner of that voice its fucking Damien, he really think he can threaten MY little girl. He's not even on my threat list, he's just a low-key gangster that'll probably die on the streets that I OWN.

It took me two hours , that's it two hours to find his little hell hole that he calls HQ , my spies told me that most of his gang was inside , great cause I'm wiping them off this earth.

Thirty minutes is all I needed to have most of his little gangsters dead and his neck in my grip. He's young, around one hundred and fifty year old and his whole gang is baby play for us. After I finish him off I go to check on my baby she got a few bruises on her face and she's crying, I lift her and walk out, once everyone that belong to me is out we burn the place down. A clear message to never mess with me or what's mine.

Sophia fell asleep on our way back home and I'm grateful for that, I need to have a chat with her tomorrow. If it was a real enemies of mine I wouldn't know where she was , it would've taken me days to find her , and they won't send me a message to taunt me they'll probably send a body part. My world is ruthless and I need to try my best and protect her my little princess.

The next morning I wake to a feeling that someone is trying to escape from bed, that someone being Sophia, she's trying her best to be sneaky but every time she moved at night I would sit up with my gun in hand ready to kill whoever is trying to hurt her.

I take hold of her waist and make her straddle my chest "Good morning baby girl" I say and she blush, she just got busted.

"Morning" she mumbles "We need to talk Sophia we can do it now or after breakfast your call" I say in a stern voice

"Now" she whispers I take a deep breath and start talking, I need to tell her why she's getting changed that she's in danger.

"Baby you know daddy got lots of enemies and they want to hurt him but since they can't get to me they hurt the people I love. And I love you very very much. You don't even know how much you mean to me , so yes I need to change you, I would've loved to wait a few years first but baby that's not an option now. I need to keep you safe so no more running away for me okay"

"You...you... Lo...love me?" she ask with a blush, of course out of everything I said she only catched the I love you part.

"Yes baby I love you and adore you, little and big I love my Sophia anyway I can get her" I say and lean up for a kiss on the mouth. She blush a pretty pink shade. "I..lo...love you too" she says and I can't help but devour her mouth this time.

TWENTY.

I talked to a family doctor so he would be present during Sophia's transformation, I couldn't wait long and had an appointment for her the next day. She's going to go under anesthesia and won't feel a thing, the changing take up to six hours and sometimes more in case of complications.

After six very very long hours , the doctor finally tell me that she made it, and she's okay there was no complications during the transformation and that she's in recovery, she won't wake up until tomorrow.

I ask to take her home, not the school my private home I own a penthouse and I want my baby to be comfortable. They let me check her out and give me her new ID

Name: Sophia Vitale Gender: female vampire Date of birth: 6/3/2996 (today's date) Category: little, 2 y old Dom: Dimitri vitale

She's mine now officially, I take her to my home I have a room all ready for her. Its pastel colors her favorite with a crib, a changing table, all the toys she can imagine, her stuffy Dumbo, pacifiers, bottles, diapers and a wardrobe full of new clothes.

She'll be in her little space for a while, she can't control her body or walk she'll need to learn how to control her body all over again. I change her clothes to a diaper, onesie that says "daddy princess" and stuck a paci in her mouth. I place her in her crib and turn the baby monitor on, she won't wake up till later tomorrow but just in case.

I was right she didn't wake up till noon, I heard her cries and went to pick her up "good morning princess" I say she tries to talk but she can't the word turned to some meaningless babble. She start crying harder "shushh baby its okay you'll be able to talk in no time soon", I change her diaper and clothes I keep her in onesies since they are comfy.

I put her in my lap and feed her a bottle, it's full of blood she's going to need lots of blood for the first week, afterward she can eat normal human food but she'll need blood every day or two. As she get older she can skip human food all together and just drink blood.

For pure vampires like me food mostly taste bland, until we get much older and it start to have a different flavor , I enjoy coffee with a lace of blood and alcohol but solid food don't tempt me yet.

She'll get fangs soon, tiny one and they'll hurt like hell, they'll grow to adult size fangs with age, but for now she doesn't need to bite anyone for blood.

The first few weeks are going to be hard and we're going to spend them here before we go back to school.

It take Sophia three days to start talking again easy words like daddy, food and love. We spend most day bonding together, I carry her everywhere she want to go, we watch tv together or she'll listen to me telling her stories about me.

Another three days and she's able to crawl , I'll leave her in front of the tv only to come find her in another room or hiding under a bed or table, she think it's funny playing hide and seek with me while my heart drop every time I can't find her. I got her a playpen for when I need to leave her alone, she cried and screamed not liking it but her tantrum only achieved her a few slaps on the bum.

During the second week we started trying to walk, she'll lean against me or a sofa and stand and take a few steps. She fell numerous times on her diapered behind well at least the diaper absorbed most of the hit.

By the end of week two she could talk normally and walk again but she got a new habit of biting. First time she bit my forearm hard then I catched her biting her toys, it then clicked that her fangs are coming and they must hurt. I got her a numbing jell for her gum.

I wanted to stay hidden in our little heaven, just me and her but I couldn't skip much more of school. People were talking, rumors about me were being spread. I'm the next boss of a very powerful family, disappearing like this after the little gangsters stunt was starting to make me look bad, rumors were I was hurt or even dead.

Since my baby was doing well, I decided it's time to go back to the outside world. But before we leave I got my baby a gift a choker with a blue diamond in it, a sign of ownership, plus it got a gps hidden in it so I can always know where my baby is.

I put it on her well I just present it as a gift no need to hint about her getting collared or bugged. I did warn her about taking it off and she nod and promise not to.

On our last night in the penthouse she's laying on the couch with her head in my lap she keep playing with the diamond pendant a new nervous habit, I slap her hand off. She decide to ask about food and going back to school.

"You can eat regular food again but you'll need a special bottle every night. You'll have a new schedule either with me or one of the family to keep an eye on you in classes" I say and she nods I know she's nervous about going back as a vampire now.

TWENTY-ONE.

S ophia POV

We're back at the school and I'm a vampire now, I got a new schedule to match what I am. My room that FYI I never slept in was changed it look like the room I slept in back at the penthouse now. I hate sleeping alone I got used to sleeping with Dimitri but for the last two weeks I would sleep like the dead and couldn't fight even if I wanted to.

Dimitri got me this choker with a blue heart pendant he said it was gift since I'm now his, but it's a choker I might be little but I'm not dumb I knew it meant I was claimed, vampires can be very possessive. I have this new habit of playing with my pendant whenever I'm nervous he keep slapping my hand always but It's really comforting knowing that someone is there for you.

After Andy and Damien kidnapping episode I needed the comfort, if I was still at home and someone kidnapped me I doubt my mother will even notice.

I got my new schedule, I had no academic classes none, my schedule was full of vampire 101 and being a little , well I guess those are more important for me to learn about now. From what I understood from daddy I was the only new vampire little in school since most doms wait till they graduate before they change their subs.

Walking down the halls I could hear tone of whispers and rumors almost everyone is looking at us , I do grabby hands at Dimitri and he carry me the rest of the way, I had breakfast in our dorm I wasn't ready to face the cafeteria yet. My first class is little activities but this one is different, I still have Miss Blair but instead of littles being alone, we get new doms who'll participate with us every day. I was hoping daddy will stay with me but he shook his head no and told me we'll have Aunt Maria today.

I saw Rory for the first time in two weeks and jumped on him trying to hug him we both fell to the floor and Maria had to lift us up, I ignored her mad glance and just giggled. Running and playing with the others was super hard for me, I got tired easily and wasn't that fast. In the second half of class I was so out of breath that I just sat with Aunt Maria and watched the other playing.

My day passed quickly, well except the many many glances I had thrown my way and rumors about why I was changed but I mostly ignored them I was used to them in my old school.

I tried hard food for dinner since my breakfast was cereal and lunch was soup. Anyways dinner is real food I had steak, mashed potatoes with some veg. Food still taste amazing thank god. After dinner I said goodnight to everyone and we went to our dorm.

I was wearing diapers the whole day since I couldn't control my bladder yet, no one made fun of me about it since it was hidden under my skirt and it's common. Daddy gave me my bath with bubbles and toys. He dressed me footie pajama and sat down to give me my bottle it had blood in it but I was full so I only drank half of it, blood make feel full like food which is still weird for me.

Daddy said it was my bed time and carried me to my room where the crib is. Uh uh wrong room I tried to squirm out of his hold but he wouldn't let go, he set me in my crib and told me to sleep.

"Nuuuuuuuuu" I screamed "Little girl it's time to sleep" he says calmly "Nu nu nu I'm not sleepy" I scream again "Don't Raise Your Voice. I said it's bed time now close your eyes and sleep " ~Dimitri "Nu nu I want to sleep with you" I try another technique "Little girls sleep in their cribs" ~Dimitri "Nuuuuuu they sleep with daddy" I oppose "Sophia daddy got some things to do. And if I put you in my bed alone you'll fall. Now close your eyes and go to sleep you got school tomorrow" ~Dimitri

I start kicking and screaming "no sleep alone", "I hate crib", "I want daddy"

I thought I won when Dimitri picked me up and went to his room, he sat on the bed. Just when I thought I won he took my pj off slid down my diaper and gave me the spanking of my life.

"When daddy " smack "says it's time" smack "for bed" smack "you go to sleep" smack smack "you don't" smack "scream" smack "yell" smack "or cry" smack smack.

He fixed my clothes and made straddle his lap while he comforted me. When I calmed down he took me to my crib and set me down I didn't dare to throw another tantrum. I just cried myself to sleep.

TWENTY-TWO.

The next day I still didn't have daddy in little activities I had Dante who wasn't a daddy but I think deep down he want a little. My ass was still sore from my punishment and I was tired.

I went to Dante and sat with him most of the period, he offered to read me a story since I was bored. He was the best story teller ever, somehow I ended up in his lap listening to him read it wasn't just me, and other littles were there too. I was too taken by the story to notice what I was doing, I was biting on his blazer sleeve, when the scary part came in the story I bit him hard. "What the fuck Sophia" he yelled at me and I jumped he's scary. His eyes were fully black and I was sobbing now too scared of him. He stood there just looking at me for a minute before he went to touch my face making me flinch I though he was going to slap me. Instead he cup my cheeks and lift my upper lip, my fangs are starting to show and they hurt I whimper when he touch them.

"They hurt" he ask and I nod my head yes, it's why I was biting on his sleeve.

"Come on let's go to the nurse I'm sure she got something for them" he tried to take my hand but I run away and hide behind Miss Blair.

He huff in annoyance and start texting someone on his phone, when whoever he's texting replied he came toward us and addressed Miss Blair. "Miss Bee I need to deliver Sophia to her daddy her teeth hurt" My teacher nod and tell me to get my stuff, I don't mind going to Dimitri class I missed him.

I go with him willingly, just when his class ended and he was going to another classroom. The teacher wasn't there yet so I ran to him and gave him a hug.

Dante explained what happened between us to daddy and I apologized for biting him before he left to his own class.

Dimitri sit me up on his desk and check my gum. "It's bloody red Sophia why didn't you say they hurt" he scold me and I just shrug.

He rummage through my backpack and get the numbing jell he's been using on me for the last week. I hate it, it taste weird. I try to get off the table and run away but he won't let me.

"El you mind holding her for me" he ask the girl I once colored with. Elise hold me down and hold both my hands while daddy forcefully put some jell on my gums I scream and cry I hated the feeling and the taste , it taste so bitter.

When he's done torturing me he tell Elise to let go , she does and give me a kiss on my head I push her away and get a pop on my thigh for it.

I don't know if I'm lucky or not but guess who's the teacher of this period. Yes you guessed right it's the Sir that I don't know his name. I really like him he's always kind to me and I seem to always tag along in his classes.

He get in and see me in all my teary majesty he give me a soft smile and congratulate me on my changing. I was so mad at daddy that I asked the teacher "sir can I sit alone" "Well usually it's up to your daddy but since you asked so nicely sure " ~sir

I sit two desks away from Dimitri I'm so mad at him, he just forced the icky tasting jell in my mouth and made the other girl hold me down.

"Today's class is about when to step back and give your sub a space" ~sir

The idiot comment started as usual, I actually enjoy his class its funny.

"When they're sick" "If they smell bad" "When you want to play videogames in peace"

"I swear....no when you force something on them or give them no choice. They'll need some time to process. Well of course it's not on any simple stuff but something major, if you force you're little to go to sleep and they fight for space you won't give it to them because it's time for bed.

Assess the situation, do they need time to process to cry or do they need a big hug or maybe a good spank. "

I was actually paying attention for the whole period I didn't know Dimitri had to think that hard about situation with me, well I don't think I just act.

"I want a thousand word essay about assessing situations and how to solve them, you can add as many examples as you want. Class dismissed" ~sir

When everyone else was busy getting their stuff I raised my hand, he gave me a funny look but said "yes little girl" and all eyes were back on me.

"Uh...hump...what's...what's your name...everyone call you sir" I say and feel my cheeks turn red , I see that Dimitri is looking at me like I grew a second head, he doesn't know what's his name either I asked before.

Sir chuckle before he answer "well aren't you the bravest little girl ever, I've been teaching at this school for the last twenty years and nobody bothered to ask. It's Sire Nicholas angel"

I nod my head and run to hide my face in daddy's chest, he hug me back and just smile at me "my curious kitten"

TWENTY-THREE.

Dimitri POV

Sophia has been doing great in her transition she changed from being human into a vampire, a young small vampire. The biting phase got worse before it got better, she did bite everyone, and everything, nothing was safe from her and her teeth. But she's finally rocking two pointy little fangs, and the itch is gone now, she's fine now. Her progress also includes her walking, and running away from me, she loves to run and hide whenever I'm not looking or if I'm busy with anything, she'd take advantage of the moment and runs, good thing she's cute, and I can't resist her kitten eyes.

We still fight over bedtime and what baby would go down to sleep willingly, she doesn't like to sleep in her crib alone, so I compromised and moved it to my room to keep her closer to me. She'll sleep in it when I need to stay up late to finish my schoolwork, if not we'll cuddle in the bed and sleep together. Sleeping with her is a big commotion, I need to hug her and tug her close to me since she moves way too much and I saved her from falling off the bed more than once.

Ever since she went through her transition, my father has been demanding to see his new daughter-in-law, I had a feeling he plan on spoiling her rotten, he always wanted a daughter, but I'm his only blood son, and most of the family members are boys, Sophia was in for one hell of a spoiling.

Today we're going to my parent's house for a barbecue party, one that's thrown for us, and I plan on introducing my baby to the whole family, well the rest of the family, the ones she hasn't met yet. I dressed her in a pink shirt that says princess since she is one with a plaid skirt along with some high-knee socks to keep with the cute princess vibes. Despite her complaints, she has a diaper on and a pacifier clipped on her shirt.

Our friends from school Dante, Victor, Maria, Tasha, Timmy Vincent and Rory are also here along with another family that Sophia isn't familiar with.

My father Adrik welcomed us at the door I got a quick hug while my baby received a full-on bear hug and a few twirls in his arm, I have never received such a warm welcome, but she's a princess she's different of course.

Sophia was nothing but polite the whole day, she's a perfect little girl, she said hello to people and smiled politely she got so well with my mother who always wanted a daughter as well. I heard my mother make shopping and girls' night plans with my Sophie I just shook my head. They'll have to confirm with both me and my father about their plans, well good luck with that, they could get me to say yes, but my father is super protective of my mother and now my little girl.

I decided to leave her in the care of my mother and decided to spend some time with my father and the rest of the family, she's safe in here and I don't have to keep an eye on her the whole time.

"You did well son, she's a perfect little princess" ~adrik

"Thank you sir" I reply with a smug smile, he gave me a playful slap on the back and laughs.

"Go put your girl down for a nap she's been yawning for the last ten minutes, we'll call you when the food is ready" ~adrik

"Thanks, dad," I say meaning it this time and go whisk my baby away to an upstairs bedroom, she's used to afternoon naps now.

"How about you take a nap little girl" I say.

"No I'm not" yawn "sleepy" yawn. ~Sophia

"Okay how about you sit with me" I take her in my arm and cradle her like a little child.

"Just close your eyes princess" I kiss her nose and she complies falling asleep immediately.

"Ya lublyu tebya printsessa" (translation, I love you, princess)

The endTURN THE PAGE, THERE'S MORE!

SEQUEL-TWENTY-FOUR.

T he beginning

It's been a year a full year since I came here, so many things have changed, I'm no more a lost sub I'm no longer a human.

The year is 2997 the world went through some major changes, vampires are now a thing.

Human aren't enslaved well maybe just a little, at the age of 16 all human get tested mentally and divided to categories: Dom/Sub, Daddy/Little, Mommy/little, Master/Pet, Master/slave.

Today is my 17 birthday well it's the mark of my me being born as human 17 years ago , but on my ID I'm not even one.

My name is Sophia Vitale, and I'm a vampire and a little, I belong to my daddy and Dom Dimitri Vitale. We both go to Doms&Littles Academy. It's a school where you learn how to be a good sub depending on your category, it's also where you meet doms. I met my daddy one year ago and I became his little princess.

It all started with me being human but well I'm not anymore, my daddy is a mafia prince, his family is well known in the crime world. Some of his enemies threatened me, and so my daddy decided it's time for me to become a vampire.

I didn't like the idea much first but after a small gang kidnapped me thinking they could get to my daddy , well the joke on them cause daddy rescued me in around five hours. I went through the change complain free.

So it all bring us to now , I'm dressed in my school uniform, a white shirt, blue tie , blue plaid skirt , with some high knee socks and converse. I'm also wearing a diaper and have a pacifier clipped to my shirt. My hair is up in pigtails, daddy did my hair this morning with some whining on my side when he pulled too hard.

I live in the school dorm with Dimitri, I have littles and vampire related classes along some academic classes, you got to know your math (yuck).

Since today is kind of special for me, I've met Dimitri a full year ago!!! A full year. True he met me when I had tears in my eyes but still thinking back to that day it was so romantic.

Anyways I was saying, since it a special day daddy decided to take me out after school, I'm skipping toward the cafeteria feeling so happy and stress free. I went with daddy to choose my breakfast, I still eat human food but I need to take special blood bottles at night to keep me strong.

A big red apple catch my attention yummy red , something shifted in me after I was changed, red food became so luscious and appealing I don't even like red apples. I tug on daddy sleeve and ask "daddy can I get an apple"

"Sure baby chose one" he say and I skip toward the fruit section taking the biggest apple ever yummy.

"You sure you can eat it all little one" daddy ask and I nod" want me to cut it for you" I shake my head violently Nooo. I want it like it is.

We walk toward our table, we usually sit with our family, and we're not blood related. But we all belong to the Vitale family it's me the family princess, Dimitri the family heir and prince. There is also Vincent he's daddy right hand and his little Rory who's also my friend. Uncle Dante who's very quiet and uncle victor who look scary but is a big softie. I used to have only one aunt , her name is Maria but now I have another one aunt Elise she's new the family , I think uncle Dante have a soft spot for her although she's also a dom.

I say my good morning and sit down, daddy is busy talking with the others something about today's plans to go to the park. I take hold of my apple I feel my mouth watering, I have little fangs they itched like hell when I first changed. I open my mouth and attack my apple, burying my fangs in the red skin, Uh Uh, I try to bite or get my fangs out but they won't budge. I keep my struggle down quite, not wanting to alert daddy about my problem.

"I think someone lost their battle against the apple" ~victor

The traitor, he always snitch on me when I skip something on my food tray or when I struggle like right now.

"Baby what happened" Dimitri ask with a confused look.

"Ibutapletuf" I mumble meaning to say I tried to bite but the apple is too tough.

He take the apple out of my mouth and I pout, he's going to cut it now, I try reaching back for it but he won't let me have it.

"I thought we got over the biting stage" ~Vincent

Yeah yeah when my fangs were growing I would bite anything and anyone because they itched, you bite your uncle's ones or maybe ten time and they won't let it go.

"She doesn't bite, she attack" ~Dimitri

We finish breakfast quietly, I skipped the apple I got too mad at it. And we went toward my first class, I got little class, I can go to full little space when I want or feel like it. I can also be a big girl, my classes these semester are about how to distinct when I need to be a little and when I have to be big.

My classes pass by quietly, people used to give me strange looks when I first got changed but they are used to it now, they also know I'm a Vitale princess so that's a plus.

I can't wait till the day pass and we get to the amusement park. I never been there before and I just can't wait.

TWENTY-FIVE.

A musement park

Finallllyyyy the day is over and we get to go!! I'm jumping and skipping in happiness today is really special.

I get to choose my clothes so I chose a blue tutu skirt and a white T-shirt and my favorite converse. I have my blue choker on, I never take it off anyway. It's a gift from daddy and a sign that's I'm taken.

Daddy get me dressed and he put my hair in a French braid, he told me I look beautiful making me blush.

We're sitting in the car me him, Vincent and Rory, Dante and Elise who decided to tag alone. I look at the lights and the games and just can't wait to get out there. Daddy try to get my attention taking hold of my hand but I'm still taken by the games, planning on what to play first.

He then hold my chin and tug to make me look at him "I'm talking to you little girl" he says in a low voice and I know I'm in troubles

"Sorry daddy" I reply and look down. He raise my face again and say "You hold my hand the whole time, if you want to play a game ask first. And if daddy say no you don't throw a tantrum or cry got it" he says setting the rules.

"Yes daddy "I say still excited to get out and play. "Sophia if you throw a tantrum or even think about crying we'll go straight home and I'll tan your ass. I'm not joking princess behave or I won't bring you here again." he says in his Dom voice and I nod meaning it this time. "Words princess" ~Dimitri "Yes daddy" I say in a low voice.

"You guys done let's go and have fun" Vincent yell and that's why he's my favorite uncle ever.

I go on every ride with Rory, we got in the cars three times since it was so much fun. We even had cotton candy, no apple candy for me after this morning attack. We'd run toward the cars and take our seat , I keep following Rory and hitting the back of his car , he scream every time I hit him and try to take his revenge on me , but he's a really bad driver he kept getting stuck next to the railing.

We did a final round with Vincent and Dimitri, the boys were so bad asses, and it was like a car chase.

We played twister next, I sat with Dimitri while Rory sat with Vincent, and we screamed and raised our hands when the wind hit our faces.

Daddy and Vincent played some other games with us but since they were so tall and buff they didn't fit in them.

"Daddy I want to go on the carousel horses" I say but he's not paying me any attention.

"Daddddyyyy" I whine and tuck on his sleeve still no answer, I try to let go of his hand but he pull me close to him and swat my thigh telling me to behave.

"Dimitriiiiiii" I scream this time he look at me and he look mad. Uh-OH.

"Yes Sophia" he says through gritted teeth, his eyes going black a sign of anger.

"Carousel horses. Pleaaase "I try to say with my best puppy eyes.

Before he got to answer me Dante came in, he looked angry too, something was wrong.

"Boss we got a situation" ~Dante "I know, let's regroup" ~Dimitri

I don't understand what's going on, I'm slipping to my little space, all I want is to play with the horses.

"Daddy me want horses peaaaase" I say full in my little space, when Dimitri look at me I do grabby hands, wanting up. He lift me off the ground and put me on his hip.

There is a guy, he's around six feet, and he got tattoos all over his arms and neck. His eyes are full of malice, he have a smirk on his face and walking toward us.

"Well well look who we got here the prince himself." he says then look at me "and the new princess...adorable" he says caressing my face. I flinch back hiding behind my daddy while he growled and his hands on me tightened.

"Solonik what are you doing here. This isn't your territory" ~Dimitri

"I just came to say hello vitale to you and your princess" the other guy said

"Solonik this isn't your territory. Leave now and I'll let you go peacefully" ~Dimitri

"I'll go vitale I'll go. Till we meet again vitale, princess" he says and leave.

Daddy is mad, who's this guy, why was he looking at me like that. His hold on me is still super tight and he walk toward the door.

"Nuuuu daddy I want to play the carousel horses" I whine and he ignore me and keep walking.

"Daddy daddddyyyyy daddddyyyyy horsssessss nuuuuuuuuu" I whine and cry, I don't want to leave.

Dimitri look at me and he look angry, he don't give in to my whining and crying. When we get in the car he snap "Enough Sophia" he scream at me and I start crying.

We leave the park and I keep whining and trashing, daddy got enough with my tantrum, he unbuckle my seat belt and take me across his lap with me facing down.

Smack smack smack. "I said enough Sophia" Smack smack smack "now quiet" smack smack.

He put me back in to my seat and let me cry alone. Once we get to school, daddy is giving orders like crazy I don't understand what's on. He walk toward our dorm change my clothes to pj and change my diaper. He put me in my crib and leave me alone, crying myself to sleep.

He go toward the living area in our room and I hear him and the others talking. I hug my stuffy Dumbo, he's a blue elephant, closer to my chest and close my eyes trying to sleep.

I hate Dimitri.

TWENTY-SIX.

B ad morning

The next day was Saturday, I didn't have any classes, usually it's one of my favorite days but after last night I don't know how I feel about it.

I woke up my eyes swollen from all the crying and my throat was soar, I looked around the room but I was alone, daddy's bed was still made maybe he got up early. I stuck in my crib till he comes and get me. I don't feel like being little anymore, he yelled at me and spanked me for no reason, all I asked for was to go on the damn horses. And what I received was a spanking and getting yelled at, that man at the park the one daddy called solonik scared me but Dimitri care enough to ask how I'm doing! Of course not, well the answer is heck no I'm scared shitless he seemed like he want to eat me alive.

I call for daddy a few time but he don't answer well, okay I try to climb over my crib it's hard and slippy. After a few trial and error I made it to the other way, I jumped down, well thanks to my new reflexes I don't break anything but it still hurt.

I didn't get a bath last night and I smell from all the running around at the park last night. I look around our dorm and see no sign of Dimitri, I go in to the bathroom and strip of my clothes, and I haven't used the bathroom in so long. Dimitri said I can be potty trained in about a hundred year I'm not sure if he's joking or serious.

I take a quick shower, it feel weird I rarely take showers anymore, but I make do. After I finished I wrap a towel around my torso, the bathroom door open with a bang and I jump with a screech.

"What are you doing here alone" Dimitri ask, his eyes are black never a good sign.

"Taking a shower" I give the obvious answer.

"And since when do you shower alone" he says and hold my arm with a bruising grip. I try to shy away buy he don't allow it. He drag me outside and start drying me with too much force, he try to put diaper on me but I fight not wanting it. Smack "behave" he growl after he smacked my butt. I feel tears pooling in my eyes but I refuse to cry, after he's done dressing me in an onesie, placing a paci in my mouth.

"What do you want for breakfast?" he ask me but I just shrug, I don't even want to eat. He give me some cereal, and get busy talking on the phone, I push my food around. After about fifteen minutes I drain my bowl in the sink, calling that I'm done, I go sit in the living room to watch some TV.

The rest of the day passed like that, daddy busy on the phone and me sitting alone either watching TV or coloring or playing with my phone.

Sunday was pretty much the same, I tried asking him to sleep with me but he said a dry no and went back to his phone.

I woke on my own Monday, it was still early, I look to Dimitri's bed and saw he's sleeping, on top of the covers still fully clothed. He's been mean to me since Friday night, something is up I know that, but what is it, I had no ideas.

An alarm went off and Dimitri wake up groggy, he get up and look at me "Morning" he mumble and go to the bathroom, I hear the shower and I sit still and wait. In 15 minutes Dimitri was ready and came to get me up, his phone started ringing.

"I can get dressed alone" I mumble "Okay call me if you need help" he say and go back to his call.

I dress myself slowly, well after being taken care of for so long, it took some extra concentration to get dressed but I succeeded. "I'm done" I say and he just nod, we start walking toward the cafeteria with Dimitri talking in another language the whole time, I didn't understand a thing.

I don't look at Dimitri, just walk straight toward our usual table and says my good mornings. "Where did you go" came Dimitri angry voice. I look up at him, what's his problem. He don't let me reply and drag on his lap, he's still yelling on the phone and I flinch but he don't seem to notice.

"Baby girl want to come with me and chose your breakfast" victor ask and I try to get up but Dimitri says something on the phone and turn to me "what do you think you're doing" he ask through gritted teeth.

"Breakfast with victor" I'm out of my head space so I skipped the uncle part.

"Fine" he says and go back to yelling, I go with victor and he let me chose pancake and some strawberries. We go back to our table and I sit next to victor he made sure I ate everything.

The bell rang signaling the end of breakfast, I start walking with Rory since we got the first class together.

Until Dimitri once again pulled my arm, what's up with him and pulling me? I just lose it and say "whattt" between gritted teeth.

He get close to me and whisper in my ear "walk away from me one more time and I'm putting you on a leash"

"I'm not a dog" I say back "Then stop acting like a spoiled pup" he whisper yell.

And drag me to class, it's going to be a very long day.